Chocolate

With Love

and

Peace

Book has been handcrafted from cover to cover,
including the watercolor illustrations by Carolee.

From Silly to Sinister

Short Story Collection

Book Two

Original copyrights © from 1997 to 2011

Compiled in 2011

ISBN: 978-1-947573-06-2

Library of Congress Catalogue Card number: 2017911535

The Carolee Collectables
Printed in the United States of America
www.crystalsforkids.org

Carolee O'Neill
http://books2c4kids.com

Acknowledgements

To all my friends and family who willingly gave of their time to edit the stories of my twelve books; patiently taught me computer jargon; shared their computer skills with Adobe InDesign and Photoshop; and guided me through the copyright, ISBN and barcode maze. I couldn't have done it without you.

From Silly to Sinister

Book Two

Short Story Collection

To:

_____

_____

From:

_____

_____

Titles

Close to the Heart

Time to Grow Up

A Bushel and a Peck

Gotcha

Beyond Hope is a Smile

Acceptance

Brain Drain

Love from a Neighbor is
Better than Cookies

Dedicated to David,

whose courage and laughter

will always be in my heart.

Close to the Heart

Chapter 1

You know how it is. You grow up in a family of four, five or six. The older kids pick on the younger ones, and so on down the line, until they get to the baby. Well I was that baby. They named me Elizabeth. By the time I became a teenager, I was pretty tired of having black and blue shoulders and my arms bent behind my back until I hollered "uncle."At thirteen the bruised deltoids made it easy to understand that I'd be getting pounded on and insulted for a long time with four older brothers and a sister who hated me. As far as the five of them were concerned, I had straight hair, I walked wrong, my legs matched those of our piano and my butt was too big. Things would get particularly ugly when my mother took me to the beauty parlor and the beautician fried my hair. My siblings could never leave that one alone. Hence the nickname, Frizzy Elizie.

Carolee O'Neill

On the flip side of the coin, I was lucky to
have grandparents who simply adored me. They
thought perfection sat on the top of my little blonde
head. Of course I believed all that stuff, so the older
kids' insults didn't carry quite the clout they had
hoped. Besides, when Grandma and Grandpa
O'Brien were around, they didn't dare rap me on
the head with their knuckles or give me spider bites.
Then it was their turn to walk on eggs shells. Thank
heaven for my grandparents, or this baby never
would've survived the claws of her older dragon
brothers and Miss Witch.

I suppose the baby of the family should
expect to be hassled like this. But one thing for sure,
it didn't prepare me for what happened down the
road. Before I tell you the whole story, I want to tell
you about my grandparents, my mother's parents
that is.

I must admit, I thought them an unusual
looking couple. Grandpa, a thin, straight-standing,
very bald Irishman, had a nose too big for his face.
Grandma towered over him by at least a head, with

very bowed legs and a pear shaped figure with most of the pear in her bottom half. I really didn't care one way or the other how they looked. It only mattered that they treated me the best and were fun to be with. I realized this at about age two—maybe two and a half, when I saw the love in my grandparent's eyes.

One Christmas, our family decided to celebrate the holiday in Chicago at my grandparent's home. Unbeknown to me a special present awaited my arrival in the form of a sled with a little box on it. Grandpa had built it that way so I wouldn't fall off, and Grandma sewed a cushion for it. That made it very comfortable. I got so excited when Grandpa asked if I wanted to go for a snow ride that night, I almost tinkled in my panties. Right off, Grandpa tucked me in with some warm woolen blankets, and wrapped my head with a heavy scarf Mom had knitted. Out we went into the sparkling snowy-night, down the sidewalk, lickety-split. I loved looking into the lights, because it made the huge flakes seem like they melted into streamers as they fell from the sky. I tried to catch some so I could throw one at Grandpa, but they always disappeared in my mitten before I had a chance.

When I got a little bigger, oh . . . maybe three or four, Grandpa would take me to the racetrack. This was a very special treat because he'd buy me a three-scoop ice cream cone before we'd take our seats by the finish line. While he read his racing form, I'd be busy licking to keep up with the melting. After he got done, we'd go over and look at the horses. He needed to tell me how to pick out good horseflesh from the not-so-good. Nobody seemed to mind telling Grandpa anything he wanted to know about their horses. I guess they were glad to share their pride with a real Irishman. Grandpa said he appreciated their input because he needed all the scoop on his favorites; then he'd be sure to pick the winners. I just picked them by color. This always seemed to make him laugh, until mine came in first.

At fifteen, I couldn't imagine ever being without my grandparents. When I heard Grandpa was sick, I didn't worry because Grandma didn't seem worried. She just kept doing her regular things, like trying to get her laundry out before anyone else or keeping the house spotless. I never quite understood why that was so important. But for some reason, something about Grandma's squeaky clean house brought out the Irish demon in Grandpa. Usually this stayed hidden behind his quiet nature and his sweet smile, except when he got behind the wheel of a car. Then the devil himself wouldn't have ridden with him.

I must admit he could be pretty creative at getting Grandma's goat. Like the morning he stood on the back porch of their flat when I wasn't much more than a wee person and hollered to grandma that Mrs. O'Raffety just took all of her clothespins off her line.

Apparently, grandma saw this as some sort of a warning because she fluttered back and forth, arms flaying in the air, like she had no idea which direction to go. After a bit she rushed to the linen closet and grabbed all the clean sheets she could carry.

Her words of wisdom probably would've shocked a little person like me but I had lived with her long enough to knew it was just grandma being grandma.

"I can't let that old battle axe beat me to the line. She'll tell all the neighbors that I don't have an orderly house," came her lament.

I looked at grandpa and could see a small devilish grin turning up the corners of his mouth.

The next thing I knew grandma flew down the basement step. I could hear water running and naturally I wanted to see what she did with those sheets.

I took a few steps down and I could see her jamming the sheets into the rinsing tub for her machine. The drama continued as she quickly put them through the machine's wringer, almost pinching her fingers in the roller. Then she plopped them in to the basket. And out the door she went.

With clothespin in her mouth and a couple in between her fingers she hung the sheets for all to see. Mrs. O'Raffety would be the one who didn't have an orderly home. Grandpa would have his Irish chuckle; however more often than not, he'd pay a dear price for his shenanigans when he got caught.

Right after Valentine's Day, I heard Mom telling Dad she had to go to Chicago and help Grandma with Grandpa. She said he was delirious. I knew Mom would be able to fix things, because she was an expert on everything.

It seemed like Mom had been in Chicago for a long time; I guess that's because we had to eat Dad's cooking. My oldest brother had just come home from WW11 when Dad decided to take the two of us to Chicago to see Grandpa. Dad had to take me along because there wasn't anybody to stay with me. In those days you had to be a pretty big kid before you'd be left home alone, like old enough to get married.

Carolee O'Neill

Late winter had marked the streets with leftover dirty snow as we drove along the highway. There weren't any freeways, just narrow bumpy roads for the long drive from West Bend, Wisconsin.

My parents usually made me sit in the front seat because I always got carsick. This time I got stuck in the back with a bowl. I guess my big brother earned that seat with fighting in a war and all. However, sitting alone in the back with a bowl only reminded me of my impending future—this was not a good idea.

Through my nausea I heard Dad say, "He's probably going to kick the bucket any time now." At first I didn't know who they were talking about, until the light at the end of the tunnel hit me like a train. My queasy stomach turned sour.

I pounded my fists against the top of the front seat and screamed. "You don't know what you're talking about. He's not going to die! He's not going to! How can you say such a cruel thing?"

I really wanted to hit both of them with the bowl, but knocking Dad out could've put me in a very precarious situation. I guess that gave them a clue as to how upset I was. Dad tried to say he didn't mean to say it like that. Right then, I didn't believe him. He said everybody dies sometime, and I needed to understand that Grandpa wasn't going to be around much longer.

Chapter 2

That weekend grabbed my heart and wrung it out like a damp rag. Grandma tried to protect me so I wouldn't see what Grandpa's illness had done to him. But I needed to see for myself. When no one was looking I peeked into his bedroom. With his back to me, his thin body stood on top of his bed, trying to pick nothingness off the walls. My eyes spilled with painful tears as he struggled. Without me realizing it, Grandma had come up behind me and placed a gentle hand on my shoulder. I must have jumped two feet. She didn't scold, though.

She just tried to explain that the lung cancer made Grandpa hallucinate.

"Please let me go in for a moment, "I begged. "I got dressed up just to see him, I even took a bath. Maybe it will make him feel better if he knows that I'm here. I might be able to make him laugh or something."

Grandma looked so sad when she said, "He's not going to know who you are, Elizabeth. He doesn't know any of us anymore. So if I let you go in and he gets upset, I don't want you to think he doesn't love you; he's very sick, sweetheart."

I stepped into the bedroom while Grandma stayed by the door. I stood in front of him, but Grandpa looked straight through me. I couldn't think of anything to say, so I asked if he needed anything. Instead of an answer, he began to pick at his bedclothes.

Then he yelled, "What's that smell? Get out of here. Go on—get out, you're choking me to death."

Heat flashed on my face. A burning pain shot outward through all of my limbs. Slowly, I backed out of the bedroom, groping for the door. Grandma quickly pulled me into her arms and led me into the living room.

"I'm really sorry, honey. I completely forgot about odors. It's just that things like perfume and cleaning products make it harder for him to breathe.

It's my fault you got hollered at," she said softly. "Try to remember that he's not himself, and that he doesn't know who he is yelling at. We need to pray for Grandpa because there's nothing else we can do."

That night I prayed that my Grandpa wasn't suffering as much as I was, watching him die.

Chapter 3

Right after the funeral, Mom helped Grandma pack. She had to come to live with us because she didn't have enough money to pay her rent. One day, Grandma asked me to come to her room.

"Honey," she whispered. "I have something that is very precious to me, and I want you to have it."

She opened her dresser drawer, and pulled out a little yellow-tinged cardboard box. She opened the lid, and I saw a gold locket. The lion's face on the front held a small diamond in its mouth and an emerald in each of its eyes. Beautiful flowing letters were engraved on the back. Grandma held it in front of me by its chain and cradled the locket with her other hand.

"Grandpa gave me this when we were first married. He had it engraved with his initials, so when I wore it he would always be close to my heart. He said the emeralds reminded him of

Ireland, and the diamond reminded him of the sparkle in my eyes. It was such a lovely gift that I made a promise to myself. I said, Mary, no matter how tough things get, you can never let this go because it's a symbol of our love for each other. I wanted Grandpa to be here when I gave it to you, but he went so fast that we weren't able to get around to it. I know he wanted you to have it. He loved you very much."

My heart welled with sadness as I looked into Grandma's eyes and promised her I would always keep it close, just like she had. She opened the locket with the tiny clasp on the side. Tan-faded photos of two little girls lay within. Grandma confirmed my mom's photo and said the other little girl had been her baby sister, Ruth.

A tear escaped from the corner of Grandma's eye, "Ruth was only a baby when she died from scarlet fever. Things were different then. They didn't have medicine that would make her better, like they do now. So we weren't able to save her."She gently turned the locket toward me, so I could see the pictures better. "Ruth was such a pretty child. You know you looked a lot like her when you were little."

"I did? Thank you, Grandma; she sure was a cute little baby. Is she buried by Grandpa?"

"No. She's over in the northwest corner of the cemetery. We were pretty poor when she died, with the depression and all. Grandpa used to walk for miles trying to find work. Most days we were just lucky to get something to eat. Sometimes all he could get was some raw meat. We'd sit on the curb and eat it, had to, before it would spoil. We were just too poor for a regular grave. We had to bury little Ruth in an unmarked pauper's grave."

Her eyes sparkled through her tears as she handed me the locket, "I know you will treasure this as much as I have. And maybe someday you'll give it to one of your little girls."

Three days after my eighteenth birthday, I had my first little girl. We lived in the same town as my parents, so I visited often. I wore the locket on my visits because it made Grandma smile when she saw it.

My mother gave me a different feeling, nothing I could put my finger on, but just a feeling.

Just before Christmas, my husband lost another job which meant we'd have to move in with my parents again. I had used the little bit of money I had set aside, trying to survive. Grandma had died the previous March from a massive stroke. The house seemed empty without her jovial hustle.

Although I did my best to keep the children quiet and out of my mother's way, she continued to be sharp with me. However, I guessed that having my family move in and out of her home every year just before Christmas was probably taking its toll. I offered to do the chores, but she wouldn't allow it. She'd just walk away saying, "Never mind... never mind."Not knowing what to do with myself, I played solitaire while the children took their naps.

Angrily, she scorned me, "Of all the things there are to do in the world, and you waste your time playing a stupid card game. Why don't you learn to do something constructive for a change?"

Confused by her outburst, I asked, "Why are you angry with me? I'm only playing a game until the girls get up. You won't let me do anything around the house. I can't play the piano unless I want to wake them up. So, tell me what it is you think I should be doing?"

Instead of offering a suggestion, she stomped out of the room. I tried various things I thought would please her, like reading the classics and knitting, but nothing worked. I finally gave up after a couple of months, hoping my husband would get a job, soon.

The whole devastating affair came to a head one morning when I walked into the kitchen wearing the locket.

"You have no right to that locket," she snapped. "I'm the one who should've gotten it. But no! You had your eyes on it for years, didn't you? You knew my mother would give it to you if you kept on her enough. How could you steal something like that from your own mother?"

I gasped. Her words were like hot pokers to my heart. My response was almost a whisper. "I was only a child when Grandma gave it to me. How could you think I would do such a thing?"

She didn't answer my question. She just stood glaring at me.

"How long have you resented me because of this locket? It's been a long time, hasn't it?"

Again, Mother didn't respond.

"I knew there was something wrong, but I couldn't put my finger on it. Why didn't you just say something? Why did you have to wait until it came to this?"

I stood staring at her with my heart banging in my chest. My words only made things worse, so I decided to stay silent. I had no place to go with my children if I left the home. I was caught between my mother's wrath and an irresponsible husband who continuously lost one job after another.

With tears running down my checks, I unfastened the locket's chain and allowed it to drop into my hand. Without a word, I held out the locket toward her. She snatched it away.

I remembered the promise I had made to Grandma to cherish it and keep it close to my heart. I hoped Grandma would understand I had to break the promise. No matter what happened, I knew I'd always have my grandparent's love in my heart. Mother could never take that away from me.

*   *   *

Years passed, but the pain didn't. Mother never said another word about the locket. On my thirty-fifth birthday, mother called. "Could you come over for a bit?"

I explained it was getting late, and I needed to get supper on the table.

"It'll only take a moment, and I'd consider it a favor if you could squeeze it in. I promise I won't keep you long."

My mother was in the kitchen making supper when I walked into the house. She turned quickly and said, "Oh, you're here already. I'll be right back. I have to run upstairs for a minute."

An uneasy sensation came over me as I stood waiting. When she returned, she reached into her apron pocket and brought out the little cardboard box the locket had always been kept in.

"I had to do this today, or I knew I'd lose my nerve," she said as she handed me the box. "I can't tell you how sorry I am I said such terrible things. I don't know what got into me. I only know we have both suffered too much because of it. I hope you can find it in your heart to forgive me."

I looked down at the locket, barely able to see it through the tears in my eyes. By the time I looked up, I saw my Mother's face twisted in pain, and wet with tears. I stood for a moment, speechless. Then I opened my arms to embrace her. We held each other, allowing our pain to melt away with our tears.

"Happy birthday, sweetheart," Mom choked out. Now we'd better get some tissues before we flood this place."

Mother lived to be eighty-eight years old. She had lots of time to spoil her grandchildren and teach them about worms and flower gardens. Every day I live I am grateful that my Mom came to me before it was too late. The locket still lives in its little cardboard box when I'm not wearing it. Grandma was right—someday I would give it to one of my little girls.

Carolee O'Neill

Time to Grow Up

With the temperature at ninety-eight
degrees, people smirked at Charlene's attire when
she stepped onto the platform in her fur coat. In
spite of their comments, she stayed poised. After
thirty-three hours on the air-conditioned train, she
had finally arrived in Valdosta, Georgia, a long way
from northern Wisconsin. The big city ran through
her seventeen year old veins, along with many
honed skills and fine breeding. How much help any
of that would be in her present situation, she had no
idea. Being six months pregnant and inconveniently
married to Bill, a PFC stationed at Moody Air Force
Base, she was sure she'd find out soon enough.

The base had been built before the Korean
conflict with little consideration for how the
families of the enlisted men would be housed.
Every day these families wandered the unkempt
tree-lined roads of the backwater town in search of
a place to stay. Often they were forced to setup
camp on roach infested ground.

To make matters worse, Charlene's mother refused to give her blessing on the marriage because of the detestable pregnancy and the social disgrace Charlene brought to the family.

Not wanting to listen to her mother's constant reminders, she took the only option open to her: she left home, naïve to the hardships that would confront her.

After two months of dragging her trunks from place to place, Charlene began to understand what people meant when they referred to Bill as "coming from the wrong side of the tracks." Charlene's family feared that two people from such different backgrounds could not survive such a marriage. Nevertheless Charlene's parents arranged for a wedding to give the baby legitimacy. Time would decide how their lives played out, as they struggled with their differences, very little food and even less money.

Most of the rooms Bill found reeked of rotten wood and a pungent stench that made Charlene's nose run. They had just left such a place.

An old bed and small dresser had been crammed into a ten by ten dank, foul smelling room with floorboards that opened to the ground.

Dragging her belongings, Charlene said concernedly, "I need to get settled soon, before my baby comes. Things aren't getting any better and I can't have a baby in the street."

"I think things will get better now," Bill said. "The landlord sounded friendly on the phone and was happy to hear about the baby."

Old southern mansions lined the street where they walked. Giant trees swagged with Spanish moss accented the age of the buildings. As they approached the corner, Bill glanced at a crumpled piece of paper with the address scribbled on it.

"It must be that one over there."

"I sure hope so," Charlene sighed.

A tattered and buckled screen-door hung from the side entrance to the house. The banister, which had surrendered to dry rot, leaned outward toward the flowering poinsettias. Bill glanced nervously at his watch; it was two in the afternoon when the couple climbed the warped stairs and walked onto the porch. Charlene tried to be hopeful, but it came hard. Bill had called ahead and the landlord said the room was still available. They knew it didn't mean a thing; somebody could've beaten them to it. If that happened, they'd be back on the street. Then a bench would be the most they could hope for. He knew Charlene would never lay on the ground with roaches as long as his middle finger.

Getting impatient for an answer to his knock, Bill tried the door and found it open. They stepped into a fairly large room which lacked adequate furnishings. Mustiness filled the air. The large, long windows were open as far as possible to let the dankness escape. Torn brown shades which looked as though they would crumble at the slightest touch, hung unevenly from their rollers. The sun, with its angular shadows, endeavored to improve the negativity by gently touching the old bed, the table, the chairs, and the rustic, knotted wooden floor.

"The landlord said there were several enlisted men and their families staying here, so you'll have lots of company. We'll have to share the kitchen and the bathroom with the other families, though."

Charlene gasped. "There's only one bathroom for all of us?"

"Yeah!"

Bill looked at his new wife, her mouth still open from the shock. "Don't think about it. It'll all work out just fine."

"I'm pregnant!"Charlene snapped. "I never know when I'll have to go."

"I'll rig up something for you, like a chamber pot."

"What's that?"

"It's like a bowl you go in and then empty it when you can."

Charlene placed her hands on her hips and frowned. "Are you telling me I'll have to walk through the halls carrying this . . . this chamber pot to the bathroom?"

Her unwavering stance coupled with the grimace on her face, told him she was more than offended. For Bill, hard times and outhouses were part of his life growing up with an alcoholic father who worked sporadically, beat his mother and supplemented their food supply by hunting and fishing.

"And then I get to stand in line with everyone else waiting to empty it? I'm sorry to inform you Bill, but this definitely will not work!"

"Don't get so excited, "Bill said curtly. "You only have to use it in case of an emergency."

Disgusted with Bill's attitude, Charlene turned to get a good look at the room. Her gaze scanned the walls and spotted a huge spider on the headboard. Its black, furry body matched the size of a tennis ball, and its long legs were boney and flesh colored. The room spun as she heard herself scream.

Seeing the spider, Bill stiffened from the horror on Charlene's face. "Just stay calm, I'll take care of it. First I'll have to find something to move it with."

Words stuck in her throat until she finally uttered, "You can't be serious."

"Well . . . I'm not going to kill him, "he said smugly. "They eat the roaches and some of these places are loaded with them. Believe me, you'll be glad I didn't."

Charlene wanted to run for her life, but she had no place to go. If she left, she'd be on the street with an army of roaches and spiders. If she stayed and Bill didn't kill it, the thing would wander throughout the room with its own agenda. Her imagination envisioned its journey, ending on top of her body.

My sister would never be able to cope with this thing. Every time she saw a bug the size of a dot, she'd jump on the bed and scream. I didn't know why, but I'd join her. As if that wasn't bad enough, she had to dig her nails into my arm with every step the bug took. Hearing our screams, poor mother would hear our screams and come to our rescue. I'll never forget how my sister would frantically point at the dot on the floor. Mother would grab it with a tissue and save the day. Nobody could possibly dispose of this monster with a simple tissue.

"Here, I'll use this." Bill held a small piece of cardboard in his hand that wasn't much bigger than the housekeeping spider.

Without a word, Charlene backed away as he walked toward the bed. Her back bumped up against the wall. Her head spun like a top to see if anything was on it. In a sweeping motion, she nervously brushed off her back while a cold chill ran from head to toe. Bill continued to slide the cardboard under the spider. Charlene put her hands over her mouth to muffle a scream.

For some insane reason, the spider allowed Bill to slide the cardboard under it.

"I'll put him over here behind the dresser. That way he'll catch the roaches and he shouldn't bother you, "he said, ignoring the look on Charlene's face. "This is the best room we've found so far. I'm going to tell the landlord we'll take it. What do you think?"

"It's the only room we've found! So what are my options?"

Weary from the heat and the long journey, she grabbed a suitcase and threw it on the bed. "It doesn't matter what I think. At least it's a place to stay until the baby comes."

The stained pinstriped mattress slouched on a bed that looked like an old swayback mare. *I dread having to sleep on this filthy mattress, especially since the spider setup its territory over here. I'll take one of dad's wool blankets and put it over it to give me some sort of a barrier.*

At ten-thirty Charlene admitted she couldn't put off going to bed any longer; but she found the thought of turning off the lights unimaginable with the spider running loose.

"Can we leave the lights on tonight or at least a night light?"she begged.

Tired, Bill's response sounded harsh. "That's really not necessary. There'll be plenty of light in the room from the street lamps. Look outside and see for yourself! There'll probably be so much we won't be able to get to sleep."Exhausted herself, Charlene didn't argue.

With the heat of the night in mind, Charlene folded the covers back to the foot of the bed, watching to see if anything moved. The outside lights blackened the corners and cast shadows throughout the room when Bill turned off the lamp. Resting on her back, Charlene knew she had to get some sleep; yet her heart continued to pound in anticipation of the known.

Just about the time she got comfortable, Charlene felt a tickling sensation go from her thigh to her ankle. Imagination flung her to a sitting position: a four-inch cockroach had just gotten off the top of her foot. A shrill scream filled the night air. Terror catapulted her on top of Bill—strength from every part of her body climaxed into her hands. Up and down she slammed him against the mattress with the powerhouse grip she had on his shoulders.

"My God," he yelled! "What's the matter with you? The neighbors will think I'm killing you."

The lamp toppled when he reached to turn it on. Breathless, Charlene told him about the roach.

"It's only a bug for crying out loud," he scowled. "Get a hold of yourself! You're going to have to put up with a lot worse than this down here. The poor thing is probably shaking in its boots. They're only looking for food, you know. With screaming like that I'm sure you scared the crap out of it and every neighbor within a mile. Now go to sleep! It's late, and I have to be to the base early."

"No! I won't go back to bed. I won't stay in this place for one more minute until you do something," she said with her arms folded stiffly across her midriff.

"What do you expect me to do? I can't catch every bug in Georgia to make you happy."

"I don't care! And . . . the lights will stay on forever—if they have to!"

004606607

"OK!"he shouted. "I guess I don't have a choice if I want to get some sleep. I'll go and get some cans for the bedposts."

He returned with four, three-pound coffee cans.

"This is what I'm going to do . . . so you understand. I'll put a can under each bedpost and then add some water to them. When the bugs try to climb up to the bed, they'll fall into the can and drown, OK? I'll check the cans in the morning and get rid of the dead bugs, so you won't have to look at them."

Charlene didn't want to agree, but did. It sounded like a reasonable solution. "I suppose it's OK . . . for now."

After he finished, she remade the bed, refused to turn off the light and they both fell asleep from sheer exhaustion.

The next afternoon Charlene asked Bill to move the dresser so she could clean behind it. Even though he felt her chore served no purpose, he pushed the dresser away from the wall. The spider dashed out, ran across Charlene's foot and stopped between the kitchen and the bedroom.

"Darn it!"Bill growled. "I forgot I put him back there."

Charlene stood frozen. The spider peered at her from less than four feet away.

"Oh, for crying out loud!"Bill snarled. "I guess I'll have to get rid of him. I can't go through this every day. Just keep an eye on him, so I know where he is. I'll go get some bug spray from the landlord."

Charlene focused wide-eyed on the spider, fearing he would move. Every detail became accented from its fat, furry body to the ends of its bony legs. She couldn't see any eyes, but she knew he had to be watching her.

A ritual of survival against death had begun. With spray in hand, Bill doused the spider. The spider ran up the side of the kitchen doorjamb; Bill would spray it and the spider would fall to the floor only to get up and try to climb the doorjamb again.

At last, the spider lay motionless with its wet, black body and boney legs sprawled on the floor.

Bill quickly left the room and returned with a broom and dustpan.

"Here!"he pushed the broom at Charlene. "Sweep him out of here. You have to get over this bug thing."

She stepped away from him, but he continued to shove the broom at her.

"I can't," she whimpered, too frightened to touch the dead spider even with a broom.

"You'll have to, because this monster will stay here until you do. I'm not moving it for you. So every time you want to go in the kitchen or to the bathroom, you'll have to step over him and look at him; not to mention having to smell him when he starts to rot. It won't get any easier, so you might as well do it now!"

Charlene stood there wanting to cry, but mostly wanting to go back to the safety of her parent's home. She knew that wasn't an option and the look on Bill's face told her she'd better not start to cry. She took the broom—one which had few sweeps left in it.

Bracing herself for the ordeal, she decided one hard whack would probably send it out of the door. She propped the door open and lined herself up to deliver the blow.

I can do this . . . I can!

With a full swing she hit the spider and watched it slide a wet streak across the floor. Unfortunately, it stopped at the door sill. Pressure built in Charlene's head and her pulse banged an alarming number.

Pleadingly, she turned to Bill, "Isn't that good enough?"

"No! I said out the door."

Considering the way the spider died, Charlene wasn't sure what else Bill would do if she refused. Slowly, she walked across the room to the dead spider, placed the broom next to it and closed her eyes. With the movement of the broom, she could feel the spider's body roll up the sill. Not feeling its weight any longer, she felt sure she had accomplished her mission, so she opened her eyes. The spider was draped on top of the sill, starting to fall back into the room.

Just my luck! In the last day, I've been assaulted by a huge roach, had to deal with a testy spouse and now this dead spider. With all that, I can't help wonder if I'll ever get the poor thing out of the house, or if it really matters. It seems to me it's a victim of circumstances just like me. The spider happened into human territory and now it's dead; one unfortunate moment with Bill and now I'm pregnant.

The thought of her sister jumping on the bed seemed rather silly all of a sudden. *I wonder what she would've done in this situation, especially without a mother to save her. I guess she'd do the same thing I'm doing—the best she could under the circumstances, and be thankful she wasn't the spider. Soon I'll be having this baby—something I know nothing about, much less raising a child. Somehow I'll have to deal with it all. It's time to grow up and grow up fast!*

Carolee O'Neill

A Bushel and a Peck

I'm Jane, the one who gets to tell you this story because I just turned seven. I'm suppose to tell you about Farmer's Markets. There weren't any back in the early 1930's and 1940's. My history teacher told me that. She said families grew their own vegetables, like we do.

With our parents' permission, my older ancient brothers pulled their wagons full of vegetables through the neighborhoods, hollering, "Cucumbers, tomatoes, cabbage, onions, carrots," or whatever we picked that week. People who weren't able to have a garden would hurry with their pennies and nickels to get our best stuff. I guess this happened during the depression years, so a penny bought a lot.

Mom, dad and our ancient siblings did the planting of our gardens. My brother Bob, he's ten, and I did the picking. Naturally, we complained a lot, we were just little kids. My dad said we were lucky because our family only had a half acre to work; some of our neighbors had a whole field.

Bob and I didn't think we were lucky at all. Besides, if the neighbors were so good at it, they were welcome to come over and do ours. Of course we couldn't say something like that or we'd end up with red behinds. It didn't matter how much we complained, anyway. Chores were part of being in a family, and they had to be done before we could do anything else.

Along with the six hundred quarts of fruits and vegetables mom canned every year, were the little cucumbers that would become pickles. During late summer, Bob and I spent a lot of time in the damp, cold basement, standing in front of a deep, concrete basin filled with water and baby cucumbers. To top it off, we were trapped by an octopus furnace that blocked our exit and a seven foot cistern that opened at the top with nothing for us to see except its blackness.

Bob would take one at a time out of the cold water and scrub it with the vegetable brush mom got from Fuller Brush. He had to pay close attention to the ends and the bumps; otherwise, a person could get a mouthful of sand as soon as they took a bite. Then the older brother, who had passed this job onto Bob, would know that Bob hadn't done a very good job. With a potential pounding hanging over his head, Bob scrubbed those cucumbers so hard the bumps about disappeared.

I had the most boring job out of the two. After Bob finished with the scrubbing, I had to stick each one several times with an old fashioned hairpin. They had to have plenty of holes before mom stuffed them in a jar; or else they wouldn't soak up enough brine and the flavor would be lost. My older sister would made sure I never forgot that.

This used to be her job and she said I better do it right. Having her down my throat meant things would be worse than what any of my brothers could think up. Girls are like that, especially sisters. At least I could pretend she was a voodoo doll while I stuck the cucumbers with the hairpin.

After two or maybe three thousand cucumbers, both of us started to get bored. We'd been working hard and there wasn't much left of summer. We just wanted to be kids before it was too late. Take a good look at my brothers to see how fast they got old.

Grabbing one of the last few cucumbers in the basin, and hoping there wouldn't be more, Bob said it felt soft.

I could feel the wheels churning in his head.

His smile turned crooked.

I knew there'd be a war. I had to do something quick before he did.

I snatched a handful of cucumbers from Bob's sink. I zinged one but I missed him by a hair and it flattened against the cistern wall.

Bob planted his right in the middle of my back and grinned.

"That's not fair," I screamed. "Mom's going to kill you for ruining my good blouse."

"You started it."

"Oh yeah!" I shouted as I jabbed him with the hairpin.

He squealed. If it's war you want, then it's war you're gonna get," he yelled.

He reached for me but I out-smarted him and headed for the stairs.

He must've pitched another one because something stung my left shoulder. Not sure what to do, I hid behind the giant octopus furnace.

I'm really scared of that thing. Its tube-like arms are big enough to suck you up and eat you for supper.

Then everything got way too quiet.

I swallowed hard.

Bob let out a deep ghoulish laugh that vibrated through the basement.

That did not make my day.

I screamed. I felt like I had swallowed my insides whole.

But I had to see where he hid. I poked my head out from behind the furnace.

A cucumber bounced off my forehead.

"I'm telling," I shouted and pitched another one. "You're going to get it good."

He continued to bellow his ghoulish laugh as he dragged his foot across the concrete floor with his arms outstretched in front of him.

Feeling like I'd never make it to the second floor bathroom, I zigzagged for the steps.

Another cucumber whizzed by just as mother came around the corner of the basement and smacked her right in the middle of her chest.

Stunned briefly, she brushed off the biggest chunks and looked straight at the guilt party.

Boy, was she mad.

I could tell because she didn't move and she wasn't saying a word.

When mother saw me behind the furnace, I hoped she'd think Bob started it all.

"What do you think you're doing down here? Certainly not your job," she scolded.

"Sorry, Mom," Bob whined. "That was meant for Jane. She made me do it, 'cuz she threw the first one."

"And that makes it right? Robert Leigh, you are three years older than your sister. I expect you to have more common sense. She's just a little girl, not to mention your sister."

When mother used the double-name thing I figured I had won. With my back to her, I pulled the sides of my mouth out with my fingers and stuck out my tongue.

I headed for the stairs.

That didn't fly.

"Oh no you don't," mother said as she caught me by the collar. "You'll finish the cucumbers with your brother, young lady. I suggest you get it done without any more shenanigans, unless you want more chores added to your list."

I saw Bob suck in his checks to keep from laughing. He said slyly, "Come little sister, let's finish what we started."

For the next hour I had to put up with Bob's grins and his ghoulish growls. I tried not to flinch, but I did.

To get even, I stuck the cucumbers harder and threatened him with the hairpin.

Being younger, and a girl, I had to figure out a way to stay ahead of the cruelty, don't you think?

There's my story and thanks to me you now know all about Farmer's Markets.

The End

PS: They found out that I started the war so I had to write this for my punishment. After they read it, I'll probably have to write something else.

Carolee O'Neill

Gotcha

It was the fourth of July, 2005. Alli had eaten her fill right down to the last hot dog, before she packed the car to head back. Wisconsin had become her new home and there were plenty of adjustments to be made.

The first thing she discovered was people actually drove the speed limit. In Indiana this wasn't the case. Almost everyone, unless they were ninety, cruised the streets of South Bend between forty and forty-five miles an hour. The reason for not getting a ticket seemed to be hidden in the Indiana plate, hanging on the back.

It took three hours to get from Wisconsin Dells to Appleton, a short trip in exchange for a fun filled day with her family. During the drive, family jokes, and s'morse were on her mind when she took the ramp off highway 39 to 54.

Without a car on the road, she somehow missed the fifty-five mile an hour speed limit. It seemed natural for Alli to continue at the seventy-five she traveled on highway 39, never thinking she might be headed for trouble. In her s'mores-land fantasy, she kept going until a patrol car appeared over the crest of a far away hill. Quickly, she glanced at the speedometer and gasped. Immediately, her foot went from the gas to the brakes. She sighed. Surely he was too far away to have picked her up on radar.

Alli prayed as the officer drove by, never glancing his way.

Then her eyes went to the rearview mirror. She glanced intermittently in the mirror to see if he would turn around and hoped he would disappear over the next hill. But at the first intersection he came to the officer made a "U" turn and came up behind her. Alli whispered, "Oh no. But his lights aren't flashing. Maybe there's a chance."

A tingle ran through her stomach, telling her, "I don't think so!"

He continued to follow her for about a mile before he flipped his switch. The tingle turned sickly. Now the world knew what Alli did.

Pulling to the side of the highway, she searched for her license and did her best to put on an innocent pretense as the officer approached the car. With all the expenses from her move, this was not an opportune time to get a ticket.

Faster than she could snap her fingers, her heart rate went well over one-hundred along with a flash of heat when she remembered the car was in her son's name. Questions surfaced in her mind, like why she would be driving somebody else's car? Perhaps that could be explained, but could she talk my way out of a ticket.

Protocol proceeded with the officer asking for her license and Alli saying, "What's the problem officer?"

Shifting his weight with hand on hip, he said, "Ma'am, you were going seventy-five in a fifty-five mile an hour zone."

"I'm really sorry, officer. I just came off highway 39. I guess the change in the speed limit didn't register. I've never had a ticket before. By the way, the car is titled in my son's name."

His professional tone softened. "Ma'am, if you hadn't been going so fast, I could have given you a warning. But at seventy-five, there's not much I can do. I know how it is when you're driving somebody else's car. You're probably not able to gauge your speed. I suggest that you use the cruise control."

Alli gulped on the officer's response, realizing his error. "Thank you, officer. That's a good suggestion."

I'm sorry, but I'll still have to give you a ticket. Your son's name, please. . . "

"I guess my guardian angel wanted me to slow down. I shouldn't be driving that fast anyway."

The officer stood wide-eyed while Alli gave him the name and wondered if she was the first person who had ever admitted to their guilt.

Without another word, he returned to the squad car.

Apprehension joined her wait.

Ten minutes later, he gave her the ticket to sign.

"I've reduced the speed to seventy. That will save you a little money. Tickets in Wisconsin are expensive."

When Alli saw the amount—one hundred and seventy dollars—she had a Jackie Gleason moment, only she wanted to scream "Uncle" instead of "Alice."Often she had told herself that if she ever got stopped, she shouldn't complain. She deserved the ticket for all the times she didn't get caught during her fifty-plus years of driving. Regardless, she grumbled all the way to highway 41.

Feeling sorry for herself, she stopped at a restaurant to get something fattening. As soon as the waitress came to the table, Alli began to complain about her hundred and seventy-dollar ticket.

"This was a terrible time for this to happen. I'm still paying for the move up here. Besides, I've never had a ticket before. Couldn't he have given me a warning? Blasted! I know I deserved it, but a hundred and seventy-dollars?

Looking into the face of this senior, the waitress laughed, and spoke these profound words.

"Boy, it sure took them a long time to catch up to you, didn't it?"

Carolee O'Neill

Beyond Hope is a Smile

Grandma O'Brien quickly made the sign of the cross before she got into the car. Laura had agreed to accompany her grandmother to her secret meeting place; now she wondered if it was a good idea, but it was too late to back out. Grandpa O'Brien would be their chauffeur as he sped through the streets of Chicago, rocking the old Hudson back and forth across the streetcar tracks. Without concern that he might end up with a paddy wagon in pursuit, he kept his foot firmly planted on the gas pedal. For an hour, Laura hung onto the door handle to steady herself while her grandmother said her rosary in the back seat.

Grandpa pulled the Hudson to the curb in front of a tall building that stood too close to the street. Laura hesitated before getting out. Trash, cigarette butts and empty liquor bottles littered the sidewalk. Not paying much attention, she didn't realize her grandfather had opened the car doors and began helping her grandmother with her parcels.

"I'll just wait in the car until you're finished, Mary," Grandpa said.

Often Laura would watch people wave or call to her grandmother when they saw her coming down the street. An ambiance encircled her, like a halo of trust. Vendors accepted her word, without a handshake. The organ grinder brought a beat to her grandma's heart that caused her to sway to his music as she wiped her hands on her apron. If ever a contest would be held on homemaking, the neighbors knew Grandma O'Brien would win hands down for her spotless housekeeping, and the succulent meals she prepared. These were the things people knew about her grandmother, but there were other qualities much more profound.

The stairwell of the tenement flaunted the naked wood-slats of years past. A shiver ran through thirteen year old Laura as she pulled in her elbows, and embraced her midriff. Not a trace of her flesh would be allowed to touch the grime smeared into the remaining plaster. Each step upward forced her gaze to rest on the next stair. As she climbed, she placed her foot to avoid the rat feces that had intermingled with dog hair and dead bugs in its corners. In expectation of what might fall on her, she turned in a small circle and looked around. Above her grandmother's head, cobwebs swept from corner to corner. A charcoal-gray substance streaked the ceiling, much like the fumes from a kerosene stove. None of this seemed to affect her grandmother, stepping where she pleased without a pause to consider the infested conditions.

As her grandmother continued to climb, a door to an apartment began to open. A lady poked her head out, put her hand to her mouth, then smiled broadly and shouted, "It's Mary, children! It's Mrs. O'Brien."

"Hello, Marge."Grandma said, "I brought you a few things."

From behind her mother a little girl peeked, grinned and then disappeared into the room.

"Here you go," Grandma said as she handed Marge the wicker basket and cotton sacks that swelled with their contents. Accepting the gifts,

Marge expressed her gratitude and backed into the room. Grandma turned to see if Laura was close behind. Seeing her, she motioned Laura into the flat without an explanation about its condition. Laura would be left to form her own impressions.

Marge set the things down on the floor and then rushed to a bucket of water in a corner, dipped a rag into it and began cleaning the three children's hands and faces so they would be presentable.

"No need to worry about that, Marge," Grandma said. "Having to haul water to the flat is hard enough. I can't imagine how tough it is to keep things clean; a real chore I'd say. By the way, this is my granddaughter Laura. I don't believe you've met her before. She's my daughter Dorothy's girl."

Marge embraced Laura's hands in hers, "No, I certainly have not. What a pleasure it is to meet you. We love your mother and your grandmother so. They are such great ladies."

"Thank . . . you," Laura stammered. "My pleasure also . . . I'm sure. It's especially nice to meet the little ones."

Trying not to judge the conditions her grandmother had exposed her to, Laura looked around. There wasn't a place to sit, except on the warped well-scrubbed, wooden floor. An old floor lamp with a tattered shade stood in the corner of a supposed living room to provide some light at night. Windows that reached high allowed the flashing neon light from the sign across the street to flaunt the availability of the speakeasy. The eight foot ceiling and walls displayed the same milieu of cracked and missing plaster as the stairwell. Someone had whitewashed the walls to provide a better environment or perhaps to help keep the family clean. A rectangular, black radio with a frayed cord sat opposite the lamp. Toward the back of the flat lay a couple of small pinstriped mattresses with pillows.

The children wiggled excitedly until their mother told them to sit down. They jumped onto the mattress closest to their mother to see what grandma brought this time.

"Now calm down, children. We mustn't forget our manners," Marge prompted gently.

Marge ran toward the back and returned with a spindled, wooden chair for grandmother to sit on and apologized to Laura for not having another. Then she knelt beside the mattress and carefully unpack the wicker basket. The children got to their knees expectantly, stretching their necks to peer into the basket and hopefully the bag. Each item withdrawn brought a smile of thankfulness from Marge and broad grins from the children. There was bread, fresh fruit, homemade cookies, canned goods, canned meats, fresh vegetables, nuts, cheese, powdered milk and a brightly wrapped gift for each child. From the oldest to the youngest, they waited in anticipation for their turn to open their little gift.

After the children cheered and jumped their approval, Marge began to unpack the cotton bag. Picking up the second item, she looked at grandma and then back to the dress she held with a tearful smile. Grandma's face whispered *I love you* as their tears met. Marge clasped the dress to her chest with one hand and extended the other. She hummed a melody, twirled and paraded across the floor like a model. The children joined her, giggling and clapping their little hands. The thrill of it all filled the room with joyous sounds that create precious moment.

Twenty years later Laura found herself in northern Wisconsin, mourning the loss of her grandmother. As Laura stood next to her grandma's casket, thoughts of what she had learned from her dear one, her wisdom, her kind heart and her unending sense of humor both comforted, and brought pain. Now those moments would only remain in her heart. Engrossed in her reminiscing, she barely felt something touch the back of her arm. She turned her swollen, tear-streaked face to see a lady wearing a funny little flat hat with a single flower bouncing on the top; the woman clutched a shiny-pink purse with her gloved hands as she stood wide-eyed and smiling. Her identity eluded Laura as she struggled with her grief.

So many relatives! I just can't remember them all. But something seems familiar about this one.

Searching for an answer, her eyes dropped to the lady's dress. *No, it can't be . . . it happened so long ago. It just can't be.*

Their eyes met. An instant flashed as memories emerged. *It's Marge, the lady who danced with her children.*

Warmth surged through Laura as she looked into Marge's smiling eyes. Marge's presence reflected her grandmother's goodness; the greatest gift she could have brought to the family. As the little flower on Marge's hat wave back and forth, they embraced their sorrow for the greatest lady they had ever known. Without a doubt, this grand lady taught them the meaning of love and that beyond hope, there is always a smile.

Acceptance

Marty jingled the few coins in his pocket: his severance pay, so to speak, an insult. As though so little could pay for what he had endured the last five years.

Marty watched the prison guard fumbled with the keys on the large, steel ring. When the tumbler finally gave up its grip on the massive prison lock, the guard pulled back on the iron-barred gate. The sound of steel rubbing against steel penetrated the silence. Marty's long awaited freedom loomed before him.

The red faced guard stood sway-backed with a plentiful stomach which hovered over his belt. He sneered and stepped aside. "We'll see how long it is before you're back in here. You're no better then the rest of these guys, Marty. You just think you are."

The snide remark caused Marty's stomach to sour and his clean shaven face to twist in anger. He wanted to lash out, but knew that wouldn't be smart. What would it accomplish anyway—more wasted years?

Five years ago, he had been incarcerated for a crime he hadn't committed, but no one cared, no one listened to his plea. Clearly he remembered his slender body being shoved through the gate five years ago and the cell door slamming behind him.

As he began his lonely journey down the deserted road, he wondered what would happen to him. He had been stripped of everything, his job, his family, his sense of decency. Today he faced a world that shunned convicts, even if they were innocent.

How am I supposed to live? Who will give an x-con a job? Let's face it, nobody really cares what happens to me. All I know is that I need to get as far away from this place as I can, even if it means walking until I drop.

Suddenly, something brushed against his pant leg. He heard a muffled, clacking sound, like stone hitting against stone. He looked down. A rock, the size of a golf ball, lay on the pavement with a crumpled piece of paper attached to it. He picked it up and removed the paper.

He read the bold printed letter out-loud, "Whoever finds this—I love you!"

Marty laughed sarcastically, "You've got to be kidding. Who'd pull a stupid prank like this? Well, it's not funny."

He took a couple of steps forward, paused, and looked at the note again. His anger kindled, he hurled the rock and the paper outward. The rock bounced repeatedly, like a stone skipping across water. The paper floated on a tender breeze as though suspended in time. "Some nut thinks he can solve the world's problems with the word love." He began to turn in circles, mocking the words on the paper as he delivered his hurtful message to the wind. "It's no use. There's nothing left to save. You're wasting your rocks."

The only response was silence.

"Why don't you answer me?"he shouted passionately as his burden choked his words. "Are you afraid to? Do you think I'm going to kill you because I just got out of that place? Well, I wasn't guilty. No! I wasn't guilty, but they stuck me there for five years, anyway. Now I have nothing— nothing left."

Marty fought back the tears that stifled his words, but finally he gave way to the despair. Heaviness filled his body. Slowly, he sank to the curb from the weight of his anguish.

He sat there for what seemed hours, crying and sobbing.

He began to fumble through one pocket after another, looking for a handkerchief, but found none.

A soft touch on his shoulder revealed a child with saddened eyes, holding a tissue.

"It's OK, Mister," she said with a gentle smile on her lips. "I love you, anyway."

Brain Drain

The fiend lurked in the corner in plain view. Intimidation whipped the user, like a weapon to maintain its control. Who could win against the addiction it provided, only the most daring.

Mary Alice's introduction to computers came painfully, like a spider giving birth to an elephant. It began in 1984 when her job forced a change in her lifestyle. To stay afloat she ventured into real estate. At that time the mechanics for her new learning experience looked like nothing more than a small typewriter. Not to be duped, she knew that no matter how small, it had power—after all, didn't it pull data from the Multiple Listing Service?

Although she worked hard to build a business; she knew a risk might be necessary to become successful. After three years of giving her money to the brokerage who employed her, Mary Alice opened her own company. In the meantime, a gentleman came into her life with expertise in huge computer systems for Miles Laboratory, a real live guru. What more could she have asked for? She had the real estate background, and the man she fell for wanted to set up all the programs she'd need for her business. What a deal!

As time went on, it became apparent that her fellow's first love was DOS, a program on death-row in the midst of Microsoft's birth. This put Mary Alice solidly between the new programs and David, the man who intended to fight to the death for his system. Her brain began to twiddle-de-dink with the DOS and Microsoft differences, each having their own pull on her nervous system. David rationalized that anyone could use a program which had been set up; it took brains to do the programming with the zeros and the ones. What did she know? She barely knew how to type and she certainly was not a contender to debate these hefty subjects.

Unfortunately, during Mary Alice's introduction, David's teaching skills left a fair amount of holes for a dummy to fill with error warnings, shut downs, and the one still alive and well, "the program is not responding."Most of the time, she didn't have a clue as to what David was talking about; she seemed to have missed a lot of zeros and ones in her training sessions. As her learning curve continued to take a nose dive to David's zeros, she convinced herself she could learn both programs and still open her own company. This philosophy led her to another study—meditation.

Losing patience with her inability to perceive his braininess, David decided to set up what he thought she'd need, like a spreadsheet. She could punch in the necessary numbers, and miraculously the program would add everything up to make her work so much easier. Heaven knows she couldn't go into business without a spreadsheet and a check balancing system.

Before long, frustration was Mary Alice's twin. She had spent so much time trying to figure out what she had to do, losing all the work in the computer—someplace—entering numbers in the wrong place, losing the entire screen, switching between different systems at David's command and balancing the programs checkbook, she decided it would be faster to do it all by hand. This did not make her new husband happy.

In spite of David's war-cry, DOS's spotlight continued to dim at the end of the tunnel as more and more baby Microsoft programs came on the market. When he left this world in 2001 for a system more to his liking, Mary Alice slid into home base with Word, not knowing much more than she did when the process began.

Despite the fact that new technology offered her a world of adventure, fear still gripped her innards with the thought of her previous learning curve. Regardless, she forged ahead to buy numerous digital products to keep herself on the merry-go-round. After much programming on her new found friends, redoing setups and some choice words, she managed to scanner some old photos of her children and edit her illustrations. The camera lovingly saved every precious photo she had given to her Dell; and when she trained with voice recognition, which she thought would be an exciting tool, words typed that she didn't realize she said, but not the ones she wanted on the page.

The last aha came when she asked a young man where she could find a flash. He laughed and said, as he started to unbutton his shirt, "It's been a long time since somebody asked me to do that."Being caught with a brain-drain, Mary Alice could only blush and squeal, "A flash drive."

She no longer worries about the "zeros "and the "ones, "because she felt relatively sure David could take care of all that on his big computer in the sky.

The question remained; will Mary Alice survive the fiend that sits in the corner?

Ah! Technology!

Love from a Neighbor is Better
than Cookies

I cried this morning, but it was a good thing. Gray skies had opened to a white Christmas, something my granddaughter would be thankful for. The brown dirt around my newly constructed home was covered with a brilliance that only the angels could have blown from the heavens. Christmas lights on homes blinked through the haze of flakes, bringing memories of snow crunching under foot, midnight Mass with carols galore and puffy snowflakes, landing softly on my face.

As I sat in my wingback chair in the living room, I watched my young neighbor laboriously push a wide-bladed shovel over his driveway. Within thirty minutes his entire drive had been cleared. Being a mature woman, I lacked the muscle to accomplish such a feat.

The challenge, as always, was at the end of the drive after the plow went through. Mounds, two to three feet high, peaked, like meringue on a lemon cream pie. Of course, I need not worry. I had a four-wheel drive Honda that could conquer any barrier. Laughing heartily, I realized I could attribute that attitude to my father.

After my older siblings were out of the house, the task of shoveling our fifty-foot driveway became mine. Inevitably, I would get to the end of the drive just about the time Dad wanted to leave. The icy barricade from the plow did not detour him: he surely could flattened it with his mighty Frazier, no matter what the depth. At warp speed, he'd backed out of the garage. The tires spun from the demand for power as he made his challenge. As the rear of the Frazier hit the bank, it stopped abruptly.

Shifting into gear, Dad pulled forward, got out, grabbed a can of sand out of the garage, sprinkling it over the pathway and was ready for another attempt. I grimaced as he came back faster than the first time. Ka-thump sounded in the frigid air. The car slammed into the packed snow and then slide forward into the tire groves. But Dad wasn't about to give up. He shifted repeatedly from reverse to drive, rocking the car back and forth enough to make a person carsick. During this process, sand catapulted in every direction, until the icy, highly-polished surface gleamed. Finally realizing his accomplishment, he got out of the car, examined the situation and got some more sand. I begged him to wait until I could finish shoveling, but he was bound to force nature to yield to the Frazier's clout. After repeated attempts, and sometimes ending up on top of the mound, he'd finally concede to the iceberg.

Recalling this experience, I'd have to find a way to clear my driveway, before I went charging out of the garage. Being new to the area, I didn't know anyone to call for help. My thoughts wandered to the snow-blower. However, it hadn't been started in years.

Suddenly, a man riding a four-wheeler with an attached plow swung into my drive. I watched mesmerized for the next ten minutes as this stranger cleared my drive. Who was he? And how did he know I needed help?

As he finished the area by my porch, thankful tears filled my eyes. I opened the front door and mouthed "thank you "over the roar of his machine "and a very Merry Christmas."

His eyes lit and a broad smile crossed his face as he nodded, "And a very Merry Christmas to you."

The End.

The Carolee Collectables

by Carolee O'Neill

Goodie RudeShoes: Series One, children 5 to 100.
Billy BitterBetter: Series Two, children 5 to 100.
Granny NeatFreak: children 4 to 100.
The Mouse House: children 4 to 100.
That Secret Part of Me: children 3 to 100.
From Silly to Sinister Short Stories:
Book One and Two.
Fiction for teens through mature adults.
Navigating the Potholes of Life:
Fiction for teens and adults
Adventure, comedy, drama.
A Reason to Dream:
Fiction for teens and adults.
Drama based on a true story.
Three versions of The Graduation.
The Graduation: A stand-alone novel.
Fiction for teens and adults.
The Graduation with Study Guide
for parents with teens, teens and adults.
The Graduation Study Guide
for those who prefer a separate copy of the guide.
Suspense, humor, insightful.
With God in Mind.
Thought provoking prose
for teens through mature adults.

Carolee can reached at: caroleeagain1934@gmail.com
http://books2c4kids.com
Carolee's books are available as paperback and as ebooks.
Thank you for your interest in my work.

Carolee O'Neill

From Silly to Sinister: A Short Story Collection

www.ingramcontent.com/pod-product-compliance
Lightning Source LLC
Chambersburg PA
CBHW061452170626
46811CB00004B/1469